Published simultaneously in the United States, Great Britain, Canada, Australia, and New Zealand in
2006 by North-South Books Inc., an imprint of NordSüd Verlag AG, Gossau Zürich, Switzerland.
Distributed in the United States by North-South Books Inc., New York.

Library of Congress Cataloging-in-Publication Data is available.
A CIP catalogue record for this book is available from The British Library.

ISBN-13: 978-0-7358-2091-3 / ISBN-10: 0-7358-2091-0 (trade edition)
10 9 8 7 6 5 4 3 2 1

Printed in Belgium

Published in cooperation with Annette Betz Verlag, Vienna, Munich

Heinz Janisch

HEAVE HO!

Illustrated by Carola Holland

NorthSouth
BOOKS
New York / London

This story is told in **twelve** sentences.
(Start counting now!)

In the **first** sentence, a cat runs

into the story.

In the **second** sentence, it cries,

In the **third** sentence, a dog and a mouse come in and look at the cat curiously.

In the **fourth** sentence, the cat whispers something into the mouse's ear.

In the **fifth** sentence, the mouse whispers something into the dog's ear.

In the **sixth** sentence, the mouse

leaps onto the cat.

In the **seventh** sentence, the cat — and the mouse — leap onto the dog.

In the **eighth** sentence, the mouse shakes its head.

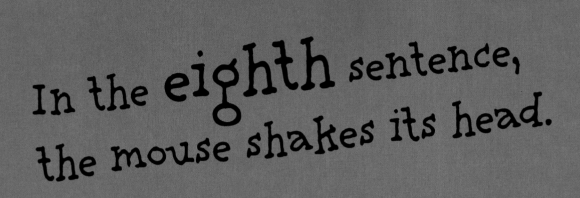

In the **ninth** sentence, the mouse cries, "Help!" and two more mice climb onto the dog and the cat.

In the **tenth** sentence, the dog
and the cat and the three mice
loudly shout,

"Heave Ho!"

In the **eleventh** sentence,
the refrigerator door opens.

In the **twelfth** sentence, a gallon of milk, a piece of cheese, and five sausages fall to the floor, and there is a pleasant dinner, at least until the twelfth

sentence **ends.**